The Berenstain Bears®
HOLD HANDS AT THE
BIG MALL

Stan & Jan Berenstain

GT
PUBLISHING

Mama Bear took Sister Bear by one hand and Brother Bear by the other as the Bear family went into the mall. "Now remember to hold hands," she said. "The mall is big and busy, and it wouldn't do to get lost."

"We'll remember," said Brother. "But what about Papa?"

"Yes, what about Papa?" said Sister. "He's not holding hands."

"I'm much too big to hold hands," said Papa. "Besides, I never get lost. Whether I'm in the great forest, the trackless wastes of the snowy mountains, or in the mall, I always know exactly where I am!"

"But the mall is big and busy — and just a little confusing," said Mama. "So if any of us *should* get lost, the Lost Cub Place is the place to go. There it is, right there."

"Look!" said Brother. "I think there's a lost cub there, now!" He was right.

"And look!" said Sister. "They gave him a lollipop!"

"I like lollipops," said Brother. "But I wouldn't want to get lost to get one."

"Do you think his mama will find him?" asked Sister.

"I'm sure she will," said Mama. "As a matter of fact, here comes his mama now."

"Come, cubs," said Mama. "We have shopping to do. Hold hands, please."
"Are you sure you don't want to hold hands, Papa?" asked Sister.

"I'm as sure as sure can be," said Papa. "Not only am I too big to hold hands, I never get lost. Whether I'm canoeing on Great Roaring River, or leading a safari across the Great Grizzly Desert, or with my family at the mall, I always know exactly where I am!"

The Bear family's first
shopping stop was at the sheet
and pillowcase store.

Mama bought some yellow
sheets and pillowcases, some
pink ones, and some blue ones.

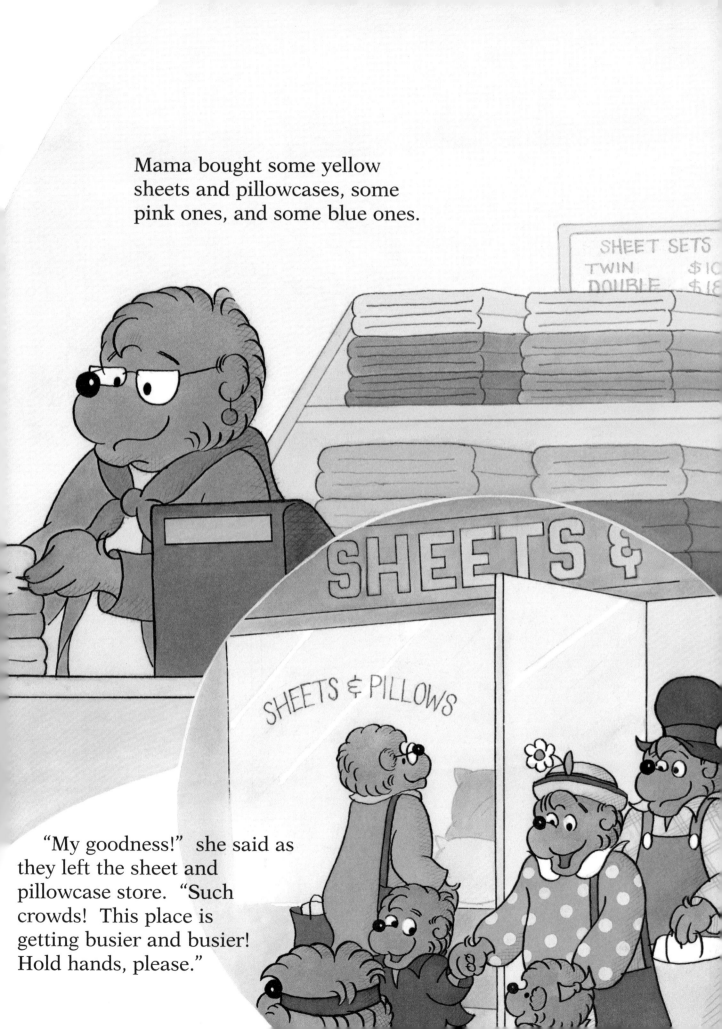

"My goodness!" she said as
they left the sheet and
pillowcase store. "Such
crowds! This place is
getting busier and busier!
Hold hands, please."

The Bear family's
next stop was at the
clothing store.

They looked at new
overalls for Papa,

a new dress
for Mama,

a new blouse
for Sister,

and a new shirt for Brother.

They looked at different colors, but they were comfortable with the old colors. So that's what they bought.

"Busier, busier, and busier!" said Mama as they left the clothing store. "Hold hands, please!"

The next stop was the honey store. The
Bears bought one jar of clover honey, one
jar of blackberry honey, and one jar of
mint honey.

"It's time to leave this busy, busy mall," said Mama as they left the honey store. "So hold hands tight and we'll try to find our way out of here." She took the cubs' hands and glanced at Papa.

"How many times must I tell you?" said Papa. "I'm much too big to hold hands. Why, I can turn around three times and still know exactly where I am. Watch!"

Papa turned around and around while Mama looked for the way out. But by the time she found the exit sign, she looked around and saw that she had lost Papa. "Where's Papa?" she asked.

"I think he got a little dizzy from turning around and wandered off into the crowd," said Brother.

"We must find him!" said Mama.

They went back to
the honey store. But
Papa was not there.

They went back to the clothing store.
But Papa was not there.

They went back to the sheet and pillow-case store. But Papa was not there. Papa didn't seem to be *any-where!*

"I have an idea," said Mama. "Come with me. But hold hands, please."
"Where are we going?" asked the cubs.
"To the Lost Cub Place!" said Mama.

Sure enough, Papa was there. He was suck-ing on a red lollipop. "Thank goodness you've come!" said the Lost Cub sitter. "He's already on his third lollipop!

LOST CUB PLACE

"And since your papa got lollipops for getting lost, I think you should get lollipops for finding him!" Brother chose green. Sister chose orange. Mama chose purple but saved hers for later.

LOST
CUB
PLACE

"Well," said Sister to Papa.
"I hope you have learned your lesson."
"What lesson is that, my dear?" he asked.
"You are never too big to hold hands."